This

Buttons Family

book belongs to

- -

- -

Cherry and Charlie and Baby Lou,

We're the Buttons, we're just like you!

And every day there's something new

For Cherry and Charlie and Baby Lou!

First published 2012 by Walker Books Ltd
87 Vauxhall Walk, London SE11 5HJ

10 9 8 7 6 5 4 3 2 1

Text © 2012 Vivian French
Illustrations © 2012 Sue Heap

This book has been typeset in HVD Bodedo

Printed in China

British Library Cataloguing in
Publication Data: a catalogue record
for this book is available from
the British Library

ISBN 978-1-4063-2858-5

www.walker.co.uk

The Buttons Family
The Babysitter

Vivian French

illustrated by
Sue Heap

WALKER BOOKS
AND SUBSIDIARIES
LONDON · BOSTON · SYDNEY · AUCKLAND

"Bella," said Mum, "meet Charlie, Cherry and Baby Lou.

Bella's come round because she's babysitting you tomorrow," Mum explained.

Cherry looked surprised.
"But Gran always babysits."
"She's busy," Mum
told her.

Bella smiled. "We'll have a lovely time."

The next night, Bella arrived after Mum had put Baby Lou to bed. Charlie and Cherry had just got out of the bath.

While they put on their
pyjamas and Mum got ready,
Dad talked to Bella.
"Here are our phone numbers,"
he said.

Charlie appeared. "Where are
you going?" he asked.
"Out for supper," Dad said.
"What about our story?"
Cherry wanted to know.
"I'll read you a story,"
Bella told her.
"Be good for Bella,"
said Mum, and kissed
them goodbye. "See you
in the morning!"

Charlie frowned.
"Aren't they coming
home tonight?"
"Of course,"
Bella said.
"But you'll
be asleep
by then.

Now, you must tell me what to do, so I get it right."

Charlie grinned. "We have midnight feasts. With cake." "And a story," Cherry added. "Hmm..." said Bella. "What about two stories for two GOOD children?" "Not pink stories!" said Charlie.

They all snuggled down on the sofa for their stories.

"**WAAAAAH!**"
It was Baby Lou.

"She wants a drink," said Charlie. "Or her teddy," said Cherry.

Bella hurried upstairs.

Baby Lou was standing up in her cot. "WAAAAH! Want Mum!"

Bella began to sing
a little song.
"Baby Lou! How are you?"
Lou stopped crying.
"Want Teddy!"

When Baby Lou was settled,
Bella finished the stories.

"Now, let's see who can make their teeth the shiniest," Bella said.

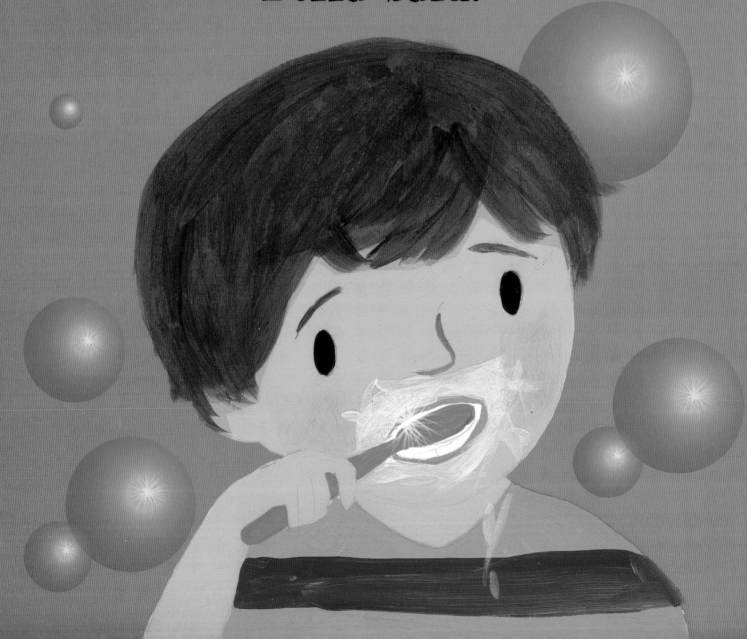

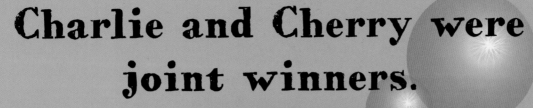

Charlie and Cherry were
joint winners.

Charlie snuggled into bed, and Cherry wriggled under her duvet. Bella gave them each a kiss, and then lay down. "What are you doing?" Cherry asked. "Staying with you until you go to sleep," said Bella, and she yawned.

Charlie went to sleep at once, but Cherry was uncomfortable. Bella smoothed her duvet, then fetched her some water.

"When you wake up, your mum and dad will be safely home." Cherry shut her eyes...

Charlie, Cherry and Baby Lou woke up early. "Hello," Dad said sleepily. "Were you good?" "Where's Bella?" Charlie wanted to know. "Can she come tonight?" asked Cherry.

"Want Bella NOW!"
said Baby Lou.

There are six **Buttons Family** books to collect.
Which ones have you read?

New Shoes

Charlie's shoes are too tight!
He says he doesn't want
new ones, but what do
his toes say?

ISBN 978-1-4063-2855-4

Going to
the Doctor

Cherry's got a nasty cold.
How will Mum persuade
her to go to the doctor?

ISBN 978-1-4063-2857-8

Staying with Gran

Cherry, Charlie and Baby Lou have
never stayed with Gran on their
own before. Will Gran make sure
they feel at home?

ISBN 978-1-4063-2860-8

First Day
at Playschool

It's Cherry's first day
at playschool and she's
feeling a little shy.
How will she settle in?

ISBN 978-1-4063-2856-1

The
Babysitter

Mum and Dad are going out.
What do Cherry, Charlie
and Baby Lou think of the
new babysitter?

ISBN 978-1-4063-2858-5

Going to
the Dentist

It's time for the Buttons
to go to the dentist!
How will they get on at
their check-up?

ISBN 978-1-4063-2859-2

Available from all good booksellers